How Is Ice Cream Made?

by Grace Hansen

Abdo

HOW IS IT MADE?

Kids

abdopublishing.com

Published by Abdo Kids, a division of ABDO, P.O. Box 398166, Minneapolis, Minnesota 55439.

Copyright © 2018 by Abdo Consulting Group, Inc. International copyrights reserved in all countries. No part of this book may be reproduced in any form without written permission from the publisher.

Printed in the United States of America, North Mankato, Minnesota.

052017

092017

THIS BOOK CONTAINS
RECYCLED MATERIALS

Photo Credits: Alamy, Getty Images, Glow Images, iStock, Shutterstock

Production Contributors: Teddy Borth, Jennie Forsberg, Grace Hansen

Design Contributors: Dorothy Toth, Laura Mitchell

Publisher's Cataloging in Publication Data

Names: Hansen, Grace, author.

Title: How is ice cream made? / by Grace Hansen.

Description: Minneapolis, Minnesota : Abdo Kids, 2018 | Series: How is it made? |
    Includes bibliographical references and index.

Identifiers: LCCN 2016962399 | ISBN 9781532100468 (lib. bdg.) |
    ISBN 9781532101151 (ebook) | ISBN 9781532101700 (Read-to-me ebook)

Subjects: LCSH: Ice cream, ices, etc.--Juvenile literature. | Ice cream processing--
    Juvenile literature.

Classification: DDC 637/.4--dc23

LC record available at http://lccn.loc.gov/2016962399

Table of Contents

Cows

Milk is the most important

ingredient in ice cream.

It comes from dairy cows!

4

Cows are milked around three times a day. The milk goes into tanker trucks. The trucks deliver the milk to creameries.

The Creamery

The creamery separates cream from whole milk. **Condensed skim milk** and cream take another trip in tanker trucks. They are headed to the ice cream factory!

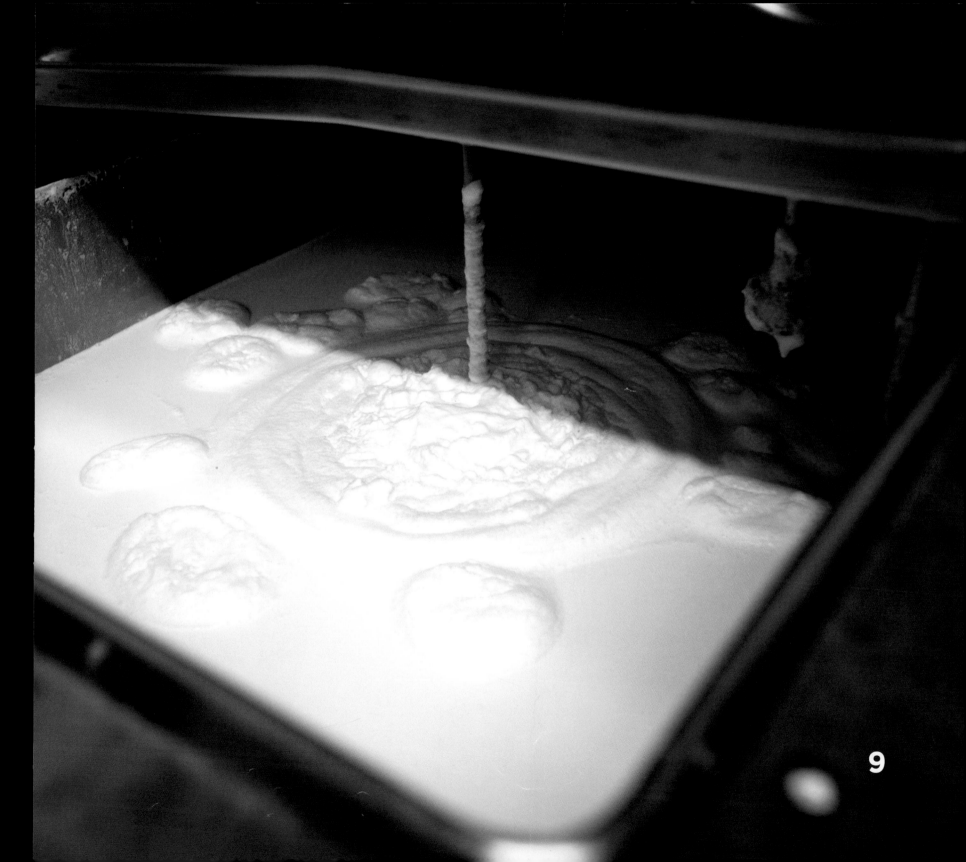

The Factory

At the factory, cream, **condensed skim milk**, and sugar are mixed together. Sometimes egg yolks are mixed in too. Cocoa powder is added here to make chocolate flavors.

The mixture is ready for pasteurization. This process kills any **bacteria** in the milk and cream.

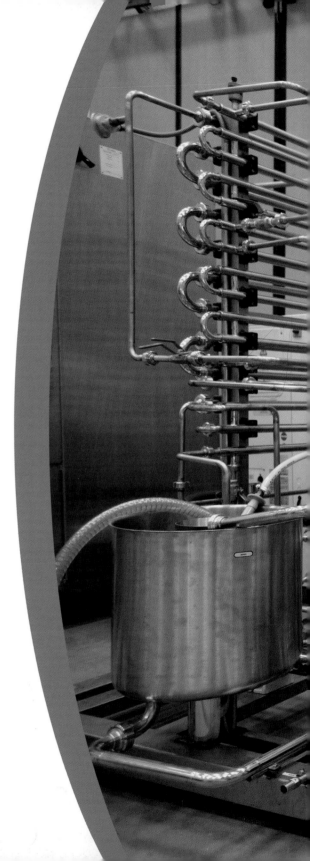

Homogenization is the next step. The mixture is put under very high **pressure**. Now the fat will not separate from the mix.

15

The mixture is now ready for flavor! Vanilla or fruit **extracts** can be added here. Peppermint and other extracts can be added too!

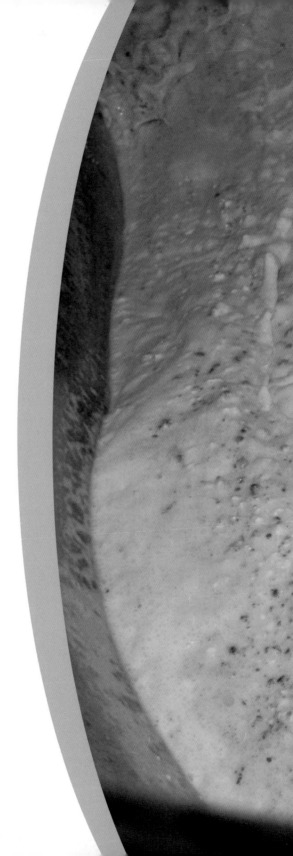

The next step is to freeze the mixture. It is pumped into a very cold barrel. The mixture is now ice cream! Ingredients like chocolate chunks and fruit can be added here.

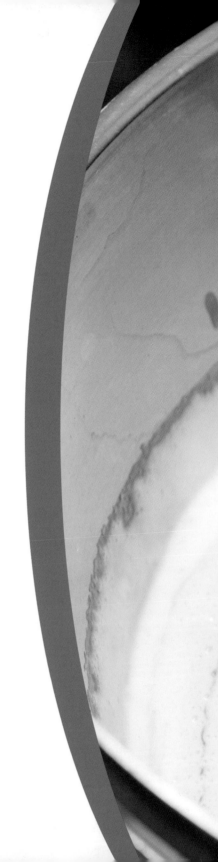

Ready to Go!

The ice cream is put into containers. The containers are placed in a very cold room. They are frozen solid. They are ready to be shipped to stores!

More Facts

- The best-selling ice cream flavors are vanilla and chocolate.

- One gallon (3.8 L) of ice cream requires 5.8 pounds (2.6 kg) of whole milk and 1 pound (0.5 kg) of cream.

- A dairy cow can produce enough milk in its lifetime to make around 9,000 gallons (34,000 L) of ice cream.

Glossary

bacteria – very small organisms that often play a role in causing illness or disease.

condensed milk – cow's milk from which water has been removed.

extract – a strong, concentrated form of a substance.

homogenize – to break up and blend the particles of fat in.

pressure – a strong force upon something.

skim milk – milk from which the cream has been removed.

Index

abdokids.com

Use this code to log on to abdokids.com and access crafts, games, videos and more!

Abdo Kids Code:
HHK0468

24